"I really liked this book because it tells you how you should care for the planet. I loved that it was Cassie's playdate because she's the shyest but keeps walking even when she's afraid."
Charlotte, age 7

"I'd love to go on an adventure like this. The conkers are so beautiful and shiny inside."
Léa

"The story was so exciting and the author described the forest so well."
George, age 8

"My favourite character is Thunder because he is so brave having only one eye."
Daisy, age 7

Katy

Chatty, sociable and kind. She's the glue that holds the Playdate Adventure Club together. Likes animals (especially cats) and has big dreams of saving the world one day.

Cassie

Shy but brave when she needs to be. She relies on her friends to give her confidence. Loves dancing, especially street dance, but only in the privacy of her bedroom.

Zia

Loud, confident and intrepid. She's a born leader but can sometimes get carried away. Likes schoolwork and wants to be a scientist when she's older, just like her mum.

Thunder

Big, white and fluffy with grey ears, paws and tail. He's blind in one eye, but that's what makes him extra special. Likes chasing mice, climbing trees and going on adventures. Is also a cat.

**Join Katy, Cassie and Zia
on more Playdate Adventures**

The Wishing Star
The North Pole Picnic
The Magic Ocean Slide

THE
GIANT
CONKER

Book Four

THE GIANT

CONKER

Emma Beswetherick

Illustrated by Anna Woodbine

ROCK THE BOAT

A Rock the Boat Book

First published by Rock the Boat,
an imprint of Oneworld Publications, 2021

Text copyright © Emma Beswetherick, 2021
Illustration copyright © The Woodbine Workshop, 2021

ISBN 978-1-78607-896-4 (paperback)
ISBN 978-1-78607-897-1 (ebook)

Printed and bound in Great Britain by Clays Ltd, Elcograf S.p.A.

Oneworld Publications
10 Bloomsbury Street, London, WC1B 3SR, England

Stay up to date with the latest books,
special offers, and exclusive content from
Rock the Boat with our newsletter

Sign up on our website
oneworld-publications.com/rtb

MIX
Paper from
responsible sources
FSC® C018072

To my mum,

for our autumns spent collecting conkers.

And to my kids,

for carrying on the autumn fun!

CHAPTER ONE

Cassandra didn't hear the doorbell ringing that Saturday morning. She was practising her street dance moves in front of her bedroom mirror, music cranked up loudly on the speaker she'd recently got for her birthday. She knew that any minute now her friends would be arriving, but first she wanted to master her high-kick-leg-hold-and-spin. It was a really challenging move and she still hadn't got it quite right.

"Cassie, turn that music off! Your friends are here!" her mum called through the door.

Cassandra had one last attempt, kicking her right leg into the air and holding on to her ankle while spinning in a circle. Finally, she did it without falling over. *Yes!* she thought, punching the air with excitement. *Just in time!*

She paused the music and charged out onto the landing.

"Wait! Can I let them in?" she cried, as she launched herself down the stairs and tried to overtake her mum. This was quite difficult, as her mum was wearing a long, colourful skirt that seemed to take up the entire width of the staircase.

Cassandra finally opened the front door and threw herself at the two girls standing on the doorstep – Katy and Zia, her absolute best friends in the world. They were all in the same class at Bishop's Park Primary, but it was out of school where the real fun happened, in their Playdate Adventure Club.

Katy and Zia staggered backwards, but were rescued by Katy's dad, who gave them both a friendly shove through the front door.

"Hi, girls! It's nice to see you," said Cassandra's mum, chuckling as the two girls edged past her into the hallway. She smiled at Katy's dad. "Thanks for dropping them round."

"No problem. Katy's been dying to have another playdate. I don't think I've ever seen them so excited as on their last one. Although I've no idea what they got up to in Katy's bedroom all that time." Cassandra could feel her friends' eyes on her. They'd made a pact not to tell anyone what *really* happened on their playdates. She hoped Katy's dad wasn't about to ask any questions.

Then: "Have fun!" he said, blowing Katy a kiss through the door. "Zia's mum says she'll be round for them after lunch."

"Mum, can we go straight into the garden?" Cassandra asked, as soon as he'd gone. "I want to show Zia and Katy my new den."

4

"OK, but put your jacket on. There's a chill in the air," said her mum. "I'll be in the kitchen. Your brother's making a mess out of his breakfast!"

Cassandra grabbed her coat and they all ran straight through to the kitchen at the back of the house. Her baby brother was sitting in a highchair, cornmeal smeared all over his face and hands. Just like Cassandra, he was a mix of their dark-skinned mother and pale-skinned father, with light brown skin and lots of freckles.

"Hey, Jonah, that looks tasty!" Cassandra laughed, ruffling his fine Afro curls and kissing him on the top of his head. "Perhaps try and aim for your mouth next time, yeah?"

Jonah gurgled, then continued to smear food around his face.

The girls tumbled out of the back door in a fit of laughter, just as Cassandra's mum walked into the kitchen with a flannel. Cassandra shut the door and grabbed hold of her friends' hands, whispering so that no one else could hear. "Just wait until you see the den. It's the perfect place to plan our next adventure!"

In the back corner of the small garden, behind a horse chestnut tree laden with conkers, was what Cassandra thought was the best den *ever*. Layers and layers of colourful fabrics were draped over the lowest branches to form a tent-like structure, held in place by Cassandra's array of multi-coloured hair clips. There was a beautiful patterned rug leading up to the entrance, edged by green conker shells, along with seashells collected on a trip to Jamaica last summer to visit her mum's family.

Inside, the den was even more spectacular. Katy and Zia gasped as they crawled through the opening, their eyes adjusting to the dim light.

More patterned rugs covered the ground and there were three rainbow-coloured beanbag cushions for the girls to sit on.

In the middle, surrounded by shiny brown conkers and crisp autumn leaves, was a small wooden table adorned with crystals and jewels, with a tiny brass tea set laid out on top. The tea set had belonged to Cassandra's grandmother, and Cassandra had played with it since she was small.

"Cassie, this is amazing!" enthused Zia. "I make dens all the time at home with my sisters, but I've never seen one like this before!"

Cassandra beamed. She was the shyest of the three girls and had felt butterflies in her tummy for days worrying that her playdate wouldn't be as good as the ones at her friends' houses. Knowing Katy and Zia loved her den as much as she did finally made the butterflies' wings stop beating.

"Where did all this stuff come from?" asked Katy.

8

"My mum's a designer. We have a room upstairs full of all these beautiful fabrics, and bits and bobs she's collected – mostly stuff from Jamaica, but these beanbags are from Egypt."

"They're really comfy," said Zia, sweeping aside her long black plait as she slumped down onto a beanbag and nestled her bottom into the soft fabric.

"So what do you think?" asked Cassandra. "Should we plan another adventure?"

Cassandra felt herself shiver with nervous excitement. On their last three playdates, it was like *actual real* magic had made their pretend adventures come to life, transporting them to space, the Arctic and the ocean. She had no idea whether the same thing would happen today, but there was only one way to find out.

CHAPTER TWO

Suddenly, a spiky green conker landed on top of the tea set, sending the cups flying. Zia leaned forwards to pick it up and pricked her finger.

"Ow!" she squealed, dropping it to the ground. "This is a dangerous conker! Where did it come from?" She sucked the tip of her finger, which had started to bleed.

Cassandra picked up the conker shell carefully and turned it over in her hands. "It must have slipped through the layers of fabric.

But I've never seen such a gigantic conker before, have you?"

The girls shook their heads.

"Why don't you break it open? Take a look inside?" suggested Katy, collecting the scattered bits of tea set and putting them back on the table in front of her.

Cassandra placed it on the floor and applied a little pressure with the heel of her trainer. At once, the spiky green shell burst open and the biggest, shiniest, most beautiful conker tumbled onto the rug.

"Wow! Can I hold it?" Zia asked.

 Cassandra picked it up and gazed at it for a second, before handing the conker to her friend.

"Amazing," Zia said, stroking the velvety brown skin with her fingers. It was the colour of rich dark chocolate, and felt smooth and warm in her hand. "Hey, I have an idea! Perhaps we could have an autumn adventure?"

"Yes, that's exactly what I've been imagining since our last playdate," said Cassandra, feeling her confidence building. "Remember at school this week when Ms Coco was talking about forests and how we need to protect them?" Her friends looked at her encouragingly. "Apparently, in places like the Amazon rainforest, there are some trees that have special *magical* properties. Imagine if there was a magical forest somewhere in the world…"

"A magical forest with one enormous conker as big as a house?" added Zia.

"That would be cool!" Katy exclaimed.

"Yes! And what if," continued Cassandra, "we went on an adventure to find it?"

Zia and Katy grinned.

13

"An autumn adventure in an enchanted forest. I love it!" Zia shrieked.

"Hold on a minute," said Katy, clasping her hand against her mouth. "Aren't we forgetting someone?"

No one answered.

"Er, you know – white fluffy coat, podgy tummy, one bright blue eye?"

"THUNDER!" Cassandra and Zia shouted in unison.

"How did we forget Thunder?" Cassandra added apologetically.

Thunder was Katy's one-eyed ragdoll rescue cat and the fourth member of the Playdate Adventure Club. He'd been a vital part of the team on their last mission to rid the ocean of plastic and had been rewarded, like the girls, with a tiny dolphin charm to hang on his collar.

"Can you call your dad and ask him to bring Thunder over?" Zia asked Katy.

Katy fiddled with the end of her ponytail and shook her head sadly. "How would we explain why we want Thunder here?"

The girls sat in silence for a moment, then Cassandra picked up the teapot and poured some blackcurrant squash into three tiny cups. "Here, drink this, it might help us think," she said, handing the cups to her friends.

Just as the girls started drinking, they heard a *scratch, scratch, scratch* from outside the den, as if something, or someone, was trying to find its way in through the fabric.

Cassandra put down her cup and went to peer through the opening.

"Katy, you're never going to believe this – look who's here!" she cried, pulling a fluffy one-eyed cat into her arms and heaving him through the narrow gap.

"Thunder!" Katy cried, burying her face into his thick white fur. "You actually came!"

Cassandra placed Thunder on the ground.

"You really do have the best cat," said Zia, stroking Thunder along his back as he nudged his body against the table. Then, grey tail in the air, he strutted proudly around the den, winking at them with his one working eye.

"Does this mean we're ready to go on our adventure now?"

"I think so!" Cassandra smiled, and Katy nodded eagerly.

The girls had a routine to mark the beginning of each new adventure. First, they got into position, holding hands and forming a circle round Thunder. Then they squeezed their eyes shut as tightly as possible.

"Imagine yourself in a magical forest," Cassandra instructed, trying to calm the fresh set of butterflies in her tummy. "There are horse chestnut trees all around you that go on and on FOR EVER, with one ENORMOUS tree – the most powerful in the forest – bearing the BIGGEST conker in the WORLD! Then repeat after me, I wish to go on an adventure."

"*I wish to go on an adventure,*" the three girls chanted.

17

After just a few seconds, they all started to experience the same fizzy, electric feeling they'd had before on their previous adventures. They felt BOILING and FREEZING at the same time, like hot and cold bubbles were shooting around the inside of their bodies. As quickly as the peculiar sensations had started, they stopped. Then the friends slowly opened their eyes.

CHAPTER THREE

"OH!" exclaimed Zia.

"MY!" gasped Katy.

"GOODNESS!" cried Cassandra in amazement.

They were still standing inside a den of some sort, but they could tell immediately it wasn't the one at the end of Cassandra's garden. It was much smaller, for a start. The girls had to hunch their shoulders and squeeze together in order to stop themselves bursting through the windows.

Either they'd massively grown, or the world around them had shrunk.

The walls were solid and built from what looked like bark, and there were two little windows with spiderwebs in place of panes of glass. The floor was covered in crunchy leaves in a rainbow of autumn colours, and there were tiny beds made of twigs and bark.

"This is the cutest house ever!" Katy whispered excitedly.

"Do you think we're inside a tree?" asked Cassandra, wondering who might live in such a small house.

"We must be. But I'm afraid I can't stay in here much longer," Zia gasped. "I'm feeling a bit squished!"

"Let's go outside and get some air," said Katy.

One by one, they crawled through a narrow opening in the trunk.

Nothing could have prepared them for what they saw outside.

They were in the middle of the most magical-looking forest. Unlike the lonely horse chestnut standing by itself at the end of Cassandra's garden, *these* trees were GIGANTIC. Their leaves were a kaleidoscope of dazzling colour, with deep oranges and fiery reds and velvety purples and opulent greens – rather like the drapes and rugs and cushions inside Cassandra's den. From their branches hung more conkers than all the children at Bishop's Park Primary could collect in a lifetime. And the forest floor was so deep in leaves and conkers that Cassandra couldn't see where the tree trunks ended and the muddy earth began.

Most incredible of all was the golden glow radiating from every tree in the forest. The air felt as though it was pulsing with light.

Cassandra glanced over at her friends and noticed that their clothes had also magically transformed. She was still in dungarees, Katy in a knitted dress and tights and Zia in a cardigan and leggings, with their coats on over the top, but they were now made of the most beautiful patterned material, again just like the fabrics in Cassandra's den. They had rucksacks on their backs and walking shoes on their feet. They were ready to go exploring!

"We did it again!" Cassandra squealed, relieved her playdate had turned into another magical adventure. "This forest is amazing!"

Zia dived down to the ground, throwing an armful of colourful leaves in the air and laughing wildly. The leaves swirled in every direction around the girls' heads, caught in the gentle autumn breeze. Cassandra and Katy joined in, tossing up piles of leaves until the air was filled with shimmering leafy confetti. Then all three girls doubled over, their arms aching, laughing so hard that their stomachs ached too.

Thunder, meanwhile, was getting buried in forest debris. He leaped up onto the lowest branch of the tree they'd crawled from moments earlier and shook leaves from his coat with a cross look on his face.

23

"When you've finished covering me in leaves, perhaps we could think about going on this adventure of yours?" he said impatiently.

On every magical playdate, Thunder amazed them by being able to speak. Cassandra wondered if the shock would ever wear off.

"Thunder, I'm sorry," said Katy, reaching up to stroke him. "We didn't mean to bury you!" She giggled. "We were just having fun. Hey, nice jacket and cool hat, by the way!"

Thunder frowned as he looked down at his new outfit, then tugged at the bobble hat on his head. "It may be fun for you," he sulked.

"Thunder's right," said Zia, her eyes turning serious now. "We should start looking for the giant conker. But which way should we go?"

The girls turned round and round, as they tried to figure out which path to take.

25

Thunder climbed further up the tree to peer out from a higher branch.

"It's that way!" he shouted, pointing with his paw.

"Are you sure? How can you tell?" asked Zia.

"Because from up here I can see a tree on top of a hill that's bigger and brighter than any other tree in the forest." Looking smug, he darted back down the trunk and hurled himself into Katy's arms with such force that she almost dropped him.

"Well, that seems easy," said Zia, laughing. "Everyone ready?"

"Yes!" said Katy, setting Thunder down.

Cassandra looked at her friends, wondering why she didn't feel quite as confident as them, especially as this was her playdate.

"Don't you think it seems a bit *too* easy?" she asked.

"What do you mean?" said Katy.

"Remember how things always *seem* to start off OK on our adventures, until we have to face some sort of challenge? I just think we need to be ready for something like that to happen today, that's all."

"And I just think you worry too much." Zia put her hand on Cassandra's shoulder. "Come on, let's go," she said, flicking her plait as she turned and walked away.

Cassandra's stomach did a nervous flip, but she didn't want to make a fuss. She found it strange that they hadn't seen or heard any other creatures in the forest and she couldn't get the little empty house in the tree out of her head. Who could it possibly belong to? Still, she joined her friends as they began to trek in the direction of the tree on the hill, crunching through the leaves.

The sun's hazy, horizontal rays filtered through the colourful trees, casting everything in amber light, and the hundreds of conkers on the forest floor gleamed a rich, glossy red. The smell of warm earth and leaves tickled the girls' nostrils as they walked. Every now and again, they would crouch down to retrieve a conker from the ground and stuff it inside their rucksacks.

I have to stop worrying, Cassandra told herself. *I'm here with my friends. We make a great team. What can possibly go wrong?*

CHAPTER FOUR

Cassandra began to relax as they carried on ambling through the forest, collecting conkers and breathing in the musty smell of autumn. With the leaves floating through the air, shimmering in the sunlight, the forest really did feel enchanted.

At times, the path disappeared among the trees and the forest was transformed into the most incredible adventure playground. Huge tree roots jutted up from the ground in tangled knots, forming structures like giant climbing frames.

The girls had to use their very best climbing skills to clamber over and under the roots, twisting their bodies this way and that to get through narrow gaps and reach for footholds and handholds. Thunder was the happiest he'd been all day, leaping and jumping with such a wide grin that he looked even more smug than usual.

After a while, the branches began to arch overhead, creating a glittering tunnel of leaves. The friends walked through it in astonishment, straining their necks as they took in the wonder of nature all around.

"It's SO beautiful!" Cassandra cried.

"I really can't believe it!" Katy agreed.

"It's like something out of a fairy tale!" Zia exclaimed.

Thunder tried not to look impressed.

But as they reached the end of the tunnel, the magic seemed to fade a little. They edged round the knotted bark of an enormous tree trunk and when they reached the other side, there was a fork in the path.

"Right or left?" Zia wondered aloud.

"Thunder, can you climb another tree and tell us which way we need to go?" suggested Katy.

Thunder sunk his claws into the bark and started to climb, just as a great SWOOSHING noise came from above. Cassandra looked up into the canopy and noticed something strange – the trees' branches were all beginning to swing round in the same direction.

"What's happening?" said Cassandra.

"Maybe it's the wind?" suggested Zia.

"But there isn't much wind," replied Thunder, from above.

"I don't think it's the wind, either," said Katy. "I think the trees are trying to show us something. Look!"

The branches had rearranged themselves so that they were clearly pointing at the right-hand path. The smallest twigs stretched out like spindly fingers to show them where to go.

"But it's the other way," said Thunder, pointing his paw in the opposite direction. "The big tree is over there. I can see the path leading straight to it."

"So why are the trees pointing to the right?" asked Katy.

"Why are the trees pointing full stop, you mean?" Cassandra replied with a shudder.

"Do you think we should just ignore them?" asked Katy thoughtfully. "If Thunder can see the path, it doesn't really make sense to go the other way."

"I agree," said Zia. "Let's go left." And without waiting for the others to follow, she ran on ahead.

"Zia, wait!" said Cassandra, jogging to catch up. "Why would the trees be pointing the wrong way? Maybe they're trying to tell us something important."

"Maybe they don't *want* us to find the tree," said Zia. "Maybe they're trying to trick us. Maybe that's the challenge."

Cassandra felt a knot twisting in her tummy. Why wasn't Zia listening to her? Creepy or not, she didn't think they should ignore what the trees were telling them.

"Why don't we follow Zia for a while and see where the path takes us?" said Katy breathlessly, as she caught up, Thunder trotting by her side. She laid her hands gently on Cassandra and Zia's shoulders. "If we're going the wrong way, we can just turn back."

"OK," Cassandra sighed. "I suppose you're right."

But as they walked on, Cassandra became more and more aware of the quiet all around them. It was a spooky quiet, like they were the only living things for miles and miles. She still couldn't hear any birds, or the scurrying of squirrels – just their boots softly shuffling through the leaves and kicking aside conkers on the path. The glow from the trees also appeared to be growing dimmer, the autumn colours fading, the forest darkening.

"Don't you think it's strange we haven't seen any animals?" she asked, breaking the silence.

"Cassie, you need to chill," said Zia.

"But how about the house we started our adventure in?" Cassandra continued. "Surely a family of animals lived there? Squirrels, maybe? Or mice?"

"I see what Cassie's saying," said Katy. "And she's right about that house. I hadn't thought of it before, but those little beds were the perfect size for a family of squirrels."

37

Just then, Cassandra heard voices whispering deep within the forest.

"Did you hear that?" she said, startled. Zia opened her mouth to speak, but Cassandra put up her hand. "*Shh*, there it is again. Listen."

They all stopped and listened this time, and a ghostly sound came whistling from beyond the trees.

There's danger ahead.

Turn back, turn back.

"There. Did you hear it?" Cassandra's voice was quivering.

There's danger ahead.

Turn back, turn back.

The girls grabbed each other around the shoulders, legs trembling. Thunder stood rigid, tail to the ground and ears pricked back against his head. The forest was growing darker by the second and as Cassandra glanced sideways at her friends, she knew they were as frightened as her. Something was very, very wrong.

We're warning you.

Turn back, turn back.

"W-w-what's going on?" she stammered.

"I have no idea," Zia replied shakily.

"Maybe we should have stopped to figure out what the trees were trying to show us," said Katy, squeezing Cassandra's hand.

"Hey, is it starting to rain?" asked Zia, as a loud PLOP sounded nearby.

"I've never seen raindrops so big before," replied Katy.

They looked up, and that's when they saw one or two spiky green conkers plummeting to the ground, bursting open on impact. But soon this turned into five, then ten, then more and more, until spiky conkers were showering down across the forest.

39

"It's not rain!" shouted Cassandra, putting her arms over her head. "It's falling conkers! RUN!"

CHAPTER FIVE

The conkers continued to pour down with no sign of stopping. The girls dived for cover inside a huge hollowed-out log, lying by the side of the path. Thunder bounded in after them and curled up on the floor, paws over his ears.

"If we're going to find that tree, first we need some kind of covering for our heads," said Zia, rubbing at her bruised arms. "Have you seen the spikes on some of those conkers?"

"You mean you still want to carry on?" said Cassandra in disbelief, staring out into the conker storm. "Even after what the trees were trying to show us? Even after the voices? Even after *this*?"

"We can't just stay here. We still haven't found the giant conker." Zia was determined.

Conkers were now pelting down so heavily that the air was roaring and the forest floor was shaking.

"But we don't have umbrellas and our hoods won't protect our heads," said Katy, sounding worried. "And what about Thunder?"

"Listen," said Zia, "I think Cassie was right earlier – when she talked about the challenge on our last mission. It wouldn't be an adventure if it was easy. So we can't give up. We *have* to find our way through the storm."

Cassandra could see what Zia was saying, but the conker storm felt different to the tests on their previous adventures. *Then* they weren't in danger of getting spiked.

"Come on – think, think..." Zia persisted. "There must be *something* nearby we can use as an umbrella?"

Everyone looked around, as if the answer would pop up right in front of them.

Then: "I'VE GOT IT!" squealed Zia, her large almond eyes growing even larger. "We're sheltering inside an enormous log – and what are logs made of?"

"Wood!" shouted Cassandra and Katy in unison.

"Right!" said Zia. "And wood is hard and strong. If I can find a way to climb on top of this log, I'm sure I'll be able to pull off some big chunks of bark for us to cover our heads with. Kind of like wooden umbrellas!"

"But how are you going to go outside without being pelted by spiky conkers?" asked Katy.

"I've already thought of that," Zia replied. "You both need to give me your rucksacks. One won't be enough, but three bags with conkers in them should stop those spikes from getting through."

One of the things Cassandra loved about Zia was her ability to come up with brilliant solutions. She shrugged off her rucksack and handed it to her friend. Taking Katy's bag as well, Zia positioned one on her head and the other two on her arms. Her friends helped her to secure them in place, using the straps as ties.

"Here, take these as well," said Cassandra, pulling some of the clips from her hair and using them to help fix the bags even more tightly onto Zia.

Once they were finished, Zia had a thick layer of padding around her head and arms – a bit like a muscly superhero.

44

"I think you're ready, Zia, but *please* be careful," said Katy.

"Of course! Wish me luck!" With that, Zia darted outside.

Neither Cassandra nor Katy could see what their friend was doing, but they could just about hear Zia as she started to climb up the side of the log. And soon they knew she'd reached the top. There was the sound of creaking and clattering and scraping and

45

scratching above their heads, then three huge pieces of thick bark came crashing to the ground. A few moments later, they were followed by a bedraggled-looking Zia.

"You made it!" exclaimed Katy, wrapping her friend in an awkward hug. It was hard to get her arms around the rucksacks.

"Are you OK?" asked Cassandra, looking Zia up and down. "You're not hurt at all?"

"I'm fine!" Zia smiled. She unfastened the rucksacks from her head and arms and handed them back to her friends. "Come on, I'll show you what to do." Zia moved to the very edge of the entrance and dragged a section of bark back inside with her foot. Then she hoisted it above her head and started walking slowly out into the storm.

"Look!" she shouted over her shoulder. The bark was curved over her head so she was completely protected from the falling conkers.

"I'm not getting spiked at all. Follow me!"

"Coming!" shouted Cassandra and Katy together, fighting to be heard above the loud rumbling of the conkers. As Cassandra stepped outside, Katy whisked a shivering Thunder from the ground and placed him snuggly inside her rucksack.

"I *hate* the rain!" said Thunder sulkily, peeping out from the top with his one working eye.

"It's not rain, silly. Come on," said Katy, hoisting her rucksack onto her back. She heaved the bark above her head, stepped out from the protection of the log and, very cautiously, followed her friends along the path.

CHAPTER SIX

Cassandra could feel the conkers thudding against the bark above her head like small battering rams. The noise as they bounced off rang through her ears, making her head hurt. But the trickiest part was wading through the mounds and mounds of conkers and shells on the ground. Right now, the comfort of her garden den felt a million miles away. This really wasn't the adventure she'd had in mind!

And then, as quickly as the storm had started, it stopped.

The girls froze, waiting to see if any more conkers were going to come raining down.

"I think it's over," said Katy, putting her bark umbrella on the ground and picking splinters out of her ponytail.

Her friends placed their pieces of bark down too.

"I hope so," said Cassandra, rubbing her tired shoulders and shaking out her arms. "I don't think I could have kept going for much longer."

"What now?" Katy asked.

Zia was about to say something when they heard rustling. They turned to see a red squirrel scamper out of some bushes and onto the path.

"Thunder, no!" shouted Katy, as the cat scrambled out of her rucksack.

Thunder jumped to the ground and darted after the little squirrel. The squirrel's eyes almost popped out of its head when it saw

Thunder hurtling towards it, and it quickly dodged away.

The two animals started running in circles round the friends. Soon, it was impossible to tell whether the cat was chasing the squirrel, or the squirrel was chasing the cat.

"Thunder, stop!" Katy shouted again. She stretched out her arms, catching Thunder mid-leap. Then she dangled him out in front of her, his large head disappearing into the fluffy folds of fat on his neck. "Look, you've scared the poor thing half to death!"

"Spoilsport," said Thunder. "I was only having fun. I wasn't really going to eat it." He smiled innocently.

The squirrel stayed frozen to the spot, trembling with shock. Then it shook itself down and sat up on its hind legs, facing the girls with a serious look on its face.

"I'm Hazel," the squirrel said shakily. "I'm here on behalf of the animals and trees in the forest."

Cassandra had forgotten that *all* animals could talk on their adventures. She was also excited to meet a red squirrel for the first time. They were *incredibly* rare.

"We know you're here to find the biggest conker in the forest. But, please, it isn't safe. Why didn't you pay attention to what the trees were telling you? Or listen when the animals warned you to turn back?"

Hazel spoke quickly, like she was in a hurry. Her ears were pricked up and her little nose twitched nervously, alert to the forest around them.

So that's where the voices came from, Cassandra thought. *At least we weren't hearing things.* She took a deep breath before stepping forwards.

"I…I'm sorry we didn't listen, Hazel. But we'd like to know – um, I mean, was the conker storm really a *warning*?"

"A warning. Definitely a warning," said the squirrel, her eyes continuing to dart about fearfully. "This path isn't safe," she whispered.

"You need to turn back!"

"But *why*?" asked Zia, scuffing the toes of her boots against the ground. Cassandra knew her friend was cross that she'd read the signs wrong.

Hazel sighed. "Because of the Great Tree, of course."

The girls exchanged confused glances.

"You mean, you really don't know?"

They shook their heads.

"The Great Tree on the hill has been standing for hundreds of years," said Hazel, eyes wide and pointing with her paw in the direction they were headed. "It's always been the biggest tree in the forest. Every year it would grow conkers   as big as coconuts. Birds would nest in its branches and animals would take shelter among its roots. The other trees would look up from the forest below, impressed by its beauty and the way it looked after the woodland creatures." She paused for a moment to take a deep breath.

"But then, one day, the tree decided it wanted to be even *bigger, greater, more impressive.* Its roots started to spread, drinking in more and more of the earth's goodness, until, slowly, all the goodness from the forest was being sucked towards it. The trees nearby started to die. And, little by little, that circle of destruction has crept further and further outwards. So, you see, as the Great Tree becomes stronger and more beautiful, it uses up all the land's richness to grow a conker bigger than any you'll ever see again, and the forest around it is dying.

We animals, insects and plants need the forest to survive."

Hazel took another big gulp of air, then hung her head in sadness.

"But how can one tree think it's more important than every other tree in the forest?" asked Zia.

"I agree," said Katy, darting Thunder a warning look as she plopped him back on the ground. "It isn't fair."

Hazel hung her head even lower.

Cassandra's insides were fizzing with anger at the unjustness of it all. "Please, is there anything we can do to help?"

CHAPTER SEVEN

"The Great Tree has been cursed by its own greed and selfishness," said Hazel, eyes glancing quickly between the girls and Thunder. "The only way to help would be to break the curse. If you can do that, the goodness the Great Tree has stolen from the forest should flow back into the earth."

Cassandra nodded, starting to feel more hopeful.

"The trouble is," Hazel continued hurriedly, "we animals don't know *how* to break the curse. We can't even get close to the tree because we've seen what happens to everything around it. It dies!"

Cassandra thought for a second. "Do you think the conker has something to do with the curse? You said there's one enormous conker – that it's *so* big we'll never see another like it. What if we could get the conker to fall to the ground like an ordinary conker? What if, by breaking the bond between the conker and the tree, we also break the curse?"

Zia stepped forwards and held Cassandra's hands. "Cassie, I'm so sorry about before. I know I shouldn't have been so pig-headed..." She lowered her voice. "I should have listened to *you* when you told us to listen to the forest. But I promise I'm listening now. And I think you're right."

Cassandra smiled. It took a lot to admit when you were wrong.

The Giant Conker

"Hazel, do *you* think Cassie's right? Do you think the answer is to break the bond between the conker and the tree?" asked Katy.

"It's definitely worth a try." Hazel was tapping one paw rapidly on the ground, her bushy red tail twitching eagerly. "If it works, you'll not only save the trees in the forest, you'll give us back our home. Now, I should go and tell the other animals about your plan. Thank you, and good luck."

She bowed her head in gratitude, then darted off and vanished back into the undergrowth.

Once again, silence descended upon the forest. The girls stood for a moment, thinking over everything they'd just been told.

Eventually, Cassandra spoke. "I suppose we'd better get on with it then," she said quietly, feeling the weight of their new responsibility.

"Of course we should," agreed Katy. "But we're doing it together this time. We're a team. Right, Zia?"

"Yes – the best team. We're the Playdate Adventure Club. Come on!" Zia wrapped her arms round her friends and together they set off again for the Great Tree.

"And you, Thunder!" shouted Katy over her shoulder. Her cat was sitting with his back to them, staring at the bushes Hazel had disappeared into. "The squirrel's not coming back, you know!"

As the girls continued on their journey, the excitement they'd felt at the start of their adventure was replaced by a sense of foreboding. Gradually, they began to see that Hazel's warnings were true. With every step, the trees seemed weaker and sicker – their glow thinning, their colours fading – until they were surrounded by what looked like miles of burned-down forest full of spindly trees and jagged stumps.

"It's terrible," Cassandra said, choking back a sob. "Like the pictures of deforestation Ms Coco showed us in class."

"I know!" Zia sniffed. "Those pictures were horrible – but seeing a forest dying for real is so much worse!"

"And those poor animals!" Katy's eyes filled with tears as she crouched down and buried her head in Thunder's creamy fur. "To think these trees used to shelter birds and squirrels and rabbits and insects and all the forest creatures!"

Gone were the glittering horse chestnut trees, the rich smell of the forest floor and the crunch of autumn leaves. Gone was the feeling of magic that had enveloped them only a short time before. They plodded on through a landscape of dead trees and dried earth, and as they walked, their limbs began to feel heavy, their minds foggy.

"I don't think I can go on much further," Katy panted. "I feel so *tired*."

"I do too," whispered Zia.

"And me," Cassandra wheezed.

Then they saw it, standing magnificent on a hill up ahead – the most beautiful, most colourful horse chestnut tree they had ever seen.

The tree stood in such contrast to the devastation and decay around it, glowing so brightly the girls had to shield their eyes.

"WOW!" Cassandra cried.

"That tree is ENORMOUS!" Zia yelled.

"How on earth are we supposed to climb it?" gasped Katy.

Cassandra looked up and up – the tree seemed to stretch all the way into the clouds. They trudged forwards – every step was an effort – until they were clambering the hill towards the Great Tree. The earth was as cracked and dry as a desert, and their boots kept kicking up clouds of dust that got into their eyes and made them cough. They staggered the final few steps. And there, hanging from a shimmering golden branch *way* up above them, was the most incredible conker they had ever seen. Hazel was right – it really was the BIGGEST conker in the world.

CHAPTER EIGHT

Cassandra gulped and touched the rough base of the tree with her hands. But there was nothing she could use to climb up to the giant conker – no low branches, no knots in the trunk.

"Let's walk round it – see if there's a way up," offered Katy. Thunder had already started trotting on ahead.

They walked and they walked, still shielding their eyes from the glare of the tree. The trunk went on and on, with no footholds or handholds in sight.

"Seventy-seven and a half steps exactly," said Katy, as they returned to the spot where they'd started. "And every way up looks impossible."

"I don't think we can do it," said Zia, for once defeated.

"I'm sorry. This was my adventure and I think we've failed." Cassandra could feel disappointment stinging her cheeks.

But Katy was stroking Thunder softly across his back. "Maybe not," she said. "Thunder, what do you say? Reckon you can get that conker off its branch?"

Thunder yawned and then stretched out his back, big bottom in the air, front paws reaching along the dusty ground.

"I suppose so," he said with another yawn. "I am awfully good at climbing trees, you know."

With that, he leaped off the ground and

started to scramble up the trunk. He climbed and he climbed, and he climbed and he climbed, until they lost him among the thick branches high above their heads.

"Do you think he can do it?" Cassandra whispered hopefully.

"Thunder can do anything!" Katy smiled. She put her arms round her two friends again as they strained their eyes to see up into the branches. They stood like that for what felt like a lifetime. Cassandra didn't even dare to breathe as they waited for Thunder to give them a sign.

Suddenly, they heard scrabbling and clawing. Moments later, bits of bark and leaves rained down on their heads.

The girls dived out the way.

"Careful, Thunder!" Katy called out, terrified he might fall. She turned to her friends with a worried look on her face. "I really hope he's OK."

67

"I've reached the conker," Thunder shouted. "It's as big as a house!"

"Can you knock it down?" called Zia.

There was a pause. "The stalk *is* pretty thick…" Thunder replied slowly. Katy could tell he was enjoying the drama. "So it's not going to be easy. I'll need to use my claws *and* my teeth. You know, some less able cats would never manage it…"

The girls looked at each other. *Come on, Thunder!* their expressions said.

"But I'll try my best. Now, you don't want to chance the conker landing on your heads. Are you out of the way?"

"YES!" the girls chorused.

They waited, and they waited some more, until they heard it – a creaking and cracking sound that got louder and louder and louder and louder…

Then: "Look out below!" Thunder yelled.

"I think he's done it!" squealed Cassandra, squeezing her friends' hands.

And Thunder had.

As if by magic, the enormous conker broke away from its branch and plummeted down, down, down to the ground, splitting open with a CRASH as it struck the forest floor.

BANG! – the golden glow from the conker flared out in a dazzling fountain of light. The girls jumped back, shielding their eyes once more, amazed to see its shimmering rays reaching out across the forest floor.

The dead and broken ground began to transform before their very eyes. When they turned back to look at what had happened to the giant conker, they saw it gradually shrinking.

It grew smaller and smaller…and smaller and smaller…until, at last, all that was left was a conker roughly the same as the one that had fallen into Cassandra's den.

"Thunder!" shouted Katy. Cassandra and Zia turned to see the cat clambering back down through the branches of the Great Tree. The tree, like the conker, was shrinking down to its original size, its golden glow bringing everything in its path back to life.

"We did it!" Thunder said, his one blue eye sparkling.

"*You* did it, you mean!" cried Katy, pulling her cat into her arms and covering his thick fur in kisses.

Thunder growled and wiped the kisses away.

Cassandra felt every part of her body fill with the same warmth that was spreading all around them. The forest had become a kaleidoscope of autumn colour – the dead and brittle trees transformed into magnificent horse chestnuts once more, bathed in magical golden light.

"It's wonderful!" Zia shouted, beaming her biggest smile, arms stretched high.

"SOOOOOOO beautiful!" Cassandra cried out, kicking her leg in the air and spinning round and round.

Just when they didn't think things could get ANY better, an army of forest creatures came charging through the surrounding trees. There were rabbits and foxes and badgers and field mice and hedgehogs and robins and sparrows and owls and hawks and bats and woodlice and bees and ants and dragonflies, gathered in celebration of their forest coming back to life.

And leading the creatures was Hazel.

71

"It worked!" the little red squirrel said. She still spoke rapidly, but her voice sounded calmer and less anxious. "You've saved our forest. You've saved our home."

The animals cheered, pawing the ground and beating their wings.

Standing shoulder-to-shoulder with her very best friends, Cassandra felt proud to have played a part in setting things right.

"We're so happy we could help you," she said, her freckly cheeks turning pink.

Hazel put her paw in the air to silence the other animals.

"We've all seen what happens when greed takes over our forest," the squirrel said wisely. "Only through sharing will a glow of happiness spread throughout the world. So now it's time to celebrate! And to say thank you properly, we'd like to invite you to a party at my home.

74

Please, will you follow us?"

"We'd be honoured," said Cassandra, linking arms with Katy and Zia.

"Even me?" Thunder asked. "I promise I won't try and eat you!" He grinned.

"Especially you!" The squirrel smiled and Katy ruffled the top of her cat's bobble hat.

Hazel led a procession of creatures back through the forest, with Cassandra, Zia, Katy and Thunder marching and cheering in time with the others. They passed the bushes where they'd first met Hazel, the log that had acted as their shelter from the conker storm, the shimmering tunnel of leaves, the playground of roots, the path that led them to where they'd started their adventure, and then...

"So this is *your* home?" squealed Cassandra. "I *knew* a family of animals lived in this tree. I'm so glad that it's yours!"

75

"You were right all along, Cassie!" Zia said. "It's a wonderful house, Hazel."

"It really is. Thanks for inviting us," added Katy.

"Any time," said Hazel, as a family of baby squirrels came scampering out to see their mum. She broke into a playful grin. "Who'd like a game of conkers?"

A huge CHEER went up. Soon the girls and all the animals were joining in with the biggest and very best game of conkers they had ever played.

Cassandra couldn't stop smiling as she heard the laughter and joyful cries around her. It was the perfect way to end what had been their most challenging adventure yet.

When everyone started to tire of swinging their conkers, Hazel disappeared into her tree. She appeared moments later with refreshments – acorn cups filled with droplets of dew and conker shells brimming with nuts, resting on trays made from bits of bark. As the animals gathered round to feast, Hazel came over to speak to Cassandra and her friends.

"We wouldn't be celebrating if you hadn't come here," said the squirrel with a smile. "You have given us back our home! But I want you to

77

know that forests and trees are responsible for more than just providing food and shelter to creatures across the Earth. They're important for the air we breathe. So, you see, protecting the forests protects us all!"

Then Hazel lowered her voice and beckoned them closer. "Here, I want you to have these," she said, handing each of the girls a glossy conker that was brighter and shinier than any they'd ever seen, almost like it was carved out of bronze.

She tucked a fourth conker into the pocket of Thunder's coat. "Something to remember us by, and to help you remember what you've learned. Not only how important our forests are to the creatures that live within them, but also about kindness. If you continue to treat others well, and if you continue to treat your planet well, you should always feel the magical golden glow of this forest around you." She took a step back, looking satisfied.

"So now your adventure is complete. Are you ready to go home?"

CHAPTER NINE

Cassandra, Katy, Zia and Thunder said reluctant goodbyes to all the forest creatures and a special goodbye to Hazel. Then they squeezed their way through the tiny door into Hazel's house.

Cassandra knew she was going to miss the forest. She was going to miss Hazel, the other animals, the conker trees and the glow of happiness that filled the air. But when she imagined her home – the den in her garden, her baby brother making a mess in the kitchen, her favourite music playing in her bedroom ready to dance to – she also knew it was time to leave.

They stood in a circle, Thunder in the middle, and squeezed their hands firmly together.

"*I wish to go home,*" they chanted, eyes shut tightly.

Cassandra started to feel the familiar mix of whizzing, fizzing sensations shooting around her body. When they faded, she opened her eyes – and breathed a massive sigh of relief.

They were still holding hands in a circle but were now sat on the rainbow beanbag cushions inside Cassandra's den, the tea set laid out in front of them, conkers and leaves decorating the colourful rugs on the floor. Their rucksacks had disappeared, and their clothes and shoes had returned to normal. Thunder was padding around the den, meowing.

"Great playdate, Cassie!" Katy grinned.

"Better than the others?" teased Zia.

"Don't be silly. *Every* playdate is special!" Katy laughed.

Cassandra beamed as she looked from Zia to Katy – two of the best friends she could ever hope for. "I'll never forget what Hazel taught us," she said, pulling her little conker from her pocket. "We need to treat our planet well, and the things that live on it. That shouldn't be too hard with you guys around."

"Cassie, your conker!" Zia gasped.

Cassandra looked down and that's when she noticed the tiny bronze conker charm in the palm of her hand.

"It's another charm!" Katy cried. "To add to our collection. Look, mine's the same."

"And mine!" Zia exclaimed.

Thunder meowed, nudging his little charm across the floor with his paw.

"Come on, let's add them to the others," Cassandra suggested. She clipped her charm onto the bracelet round her wrist, next to the ones she'd come home with on previous adventures. Now the conker charm was nestled next to the star, the snowflake and the dolphin. Katy leaned forwards and fastened Thunder's onto his collar.

Just then, Cassandra's mum poked her head through the gap in the canopy.

"You girls OK?" She smiled her large smile. "You've been in here a very long time. Aren't you getting cold?"

"Er, we're good, thanks, Mum," Cassandra said, tugging her sleeve down over her bracelet while Katy moved to hide Thunder from view.

"Ready for lunch?"

"Um, yes, thanks. We'll be in soon."

This seemed to do the trick because her mum nodded and turned to leave.

"Phew, that was close!" said Cassandra.

Katy and Zia smiled, just as Thunder batted the conker that had started off the whole adventure towards their feet.

"What is it, Thunder?" asked Katy.

Thunder nudged the conker closer still.

85

"You want us to do something with this conker?" she continued.

Thunder meowed and kept staring up at them with his bright blue eye.

"Hey, I know!" Cassie said. "How about we take this conker into school for show and tell? We can tell our class all about the importance of trees!"

"And why we need to save them," Katy added.

"And what we can do to help!" said Zia.

"Exactly!" Cassandra picked up the conker and tucked it snuggly in her coat pocket, then ducked through the opening of the den.

"That's what I love most about our adventures," she

said, as her friends followed her across the garden towards the house. "We get to help save the world, one small step at a time!"

**How to Plan Your Own
Playdate Adventure**

1. Decide where you would like to go on your adventure.

2. Plan how you would get there. Do you need to build anything or imagine yourself in a new land?

3. Imagine what exciting or challenging things might happen on your adventure.

4. Decide if you are going to learn anything from your adventure.

5. Most important of all, remember to have fun!

FORESTS

Did you know…?

Around 30% of the Earth's land is covered in forest.

On land, 80% of known plant and animal species can be found in forests. A square kilometre of tropical rainforest may be home to more than 1,000 species.

Trees release oxygen, so forests are important to the air we breathe. They also provide us with shelter, water, food and fuel.

One and a half acres of rainforest is destroyed every second, equivalent to the loss of thirty-six football pitches every minute.

This is known as deforestation. If deforestation continues at its current rate, it will take less than one hundred years for all rainforests to be destroyed.

Agriculture, along with cattle farming, is the main cause of deforestation. A rise in demand for beef means large areas of forest are cleared to make way for cattle and the crops that are needed to feed them.

As well as destroying important habitats, because trees absorb carbon dioxide, deforestation results in an increase in carbon dioxide into the atmosphere – one of the main causes of climate change.

There are many things you can do to try and discourage the amount of deforestation:

🍂 Pick products that require less packaging.

🍂 Reuse paper and plastic bags.

🍂 Support eco-friendly companies.

🍂 Be active and plant trees – in your home or even at school.

🍂 Eat less meat to reduce the amount of animal farming.

🍂 Learn more about deforestation and help spread the word!

Emma Beswetherick is the mother of two young children and wanted to write exciting, inspirational and enabling adventure stories to share with them. Emma works in publishing and lives in south-west London with her family and two ragdoll cats, one of whom was the inspiration for Thunder. *The Giant Conker* is her fourth book.

Find her at: emmabeswetherick.com

Anna Woodbine is an independent book designer and illustrator based in the hills near Bath. She works on all sorts of book covers from children's to adult's, classics to crime, memoirs to meditation. She takes her tea with a dash of milk (Earl Grey, always), loves the wind in her face, comfortable shoes and that lovely damp smell after it's rained.

Find her at: thewoodbineworkshop.co.uk

If you loved this story, then you will love:

THE WISHING STAR

Katy, Cassie and Zia find themselves transported into outer space when their rocket made out of recycled waste magically becomes life-sized.

THE NORTH POLE PICNIC

In this icy adventure, the girls come face-to-face with Arctic animals and learn what happens when the North Pole begins to melt.

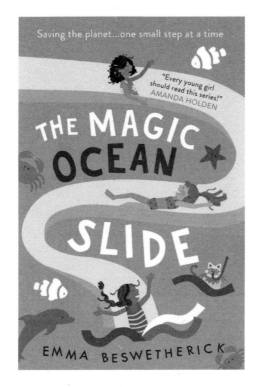

THE MAGIC OCEAN SLIDE

Katy, Cassie, Zia and Thunder discover an underwater world and learn there is more to the ocean than meets the eye!

JOIN THE CONVERSATION ONLINE!

Follow us for a behind-the-scenes
look at our books. There'll be exclusive
content and giveaways galore!
You can access learning resources here:
oneworld-publications.com/rtb
Find us on YouTube
as Oneworld Publications
or on Facebook @oneworldpublications
or on Twitter and Instagram as
@Rocktheboatnews